THE WINTER WIFE

THE WINTER WIFE

An Abenaki Folktale

Retold by
Anne Eliot Crompton

Illustrated by
Robert Andrew Parker

An Atlantic Monthly Press Book
Little, Brown and Company
BOSTON   TORONTO

FIRST EDITION

T 04/75

Library of Congress Cataloging in Publication Data

Crompton, Anne Eliot.
    The winter wife.

    "An Atlantic Monthly Press book."

    [1. Indians of North America — Legends]   I. Parker, Robert Andrew, illus.   II. Title.
PZ8.1.C882Wi   398.2′09701   74-19061
ISBN 0-316-16143-8

ATLANTIC–LITTLE, BROWN BOOKS
ARE PUBLISHED BY
LITTLE, BROWN AND COMPANY
IN ASSOCIATION WITH
THE ATLANTIC MONTHLY PRESS

Published simultaneously in Canada
by Little, Brown & Company (Canada) Limited

PRINTED IN THE UNITED STATES OF AMERICA

THE WINTER WIFE

A HUNTER lived alone in the winter woods. He trapped fur to trade. He hunted for his meat.

One day he found a moose track in the snow. Joyfully, he followed this track. The meat of one moose would last him all winter.

The track was stale, the snow did not sparkle. The hunter knew the moose was far ahead so he walked carelessly. His snowshoes creaked and crunched.

He came to a tree that the moose had stripped of bark. He came to the moose's snow bed. He stooped to look for fresh sparkle in the tracks.

A crash in the bushes startled him. He looked up and saw a young cow moose trotting away.

He cried out, knowing he could not catch her now. But to his surprise, she stopped and turned. She looked back at him, long and hard, almost as if she could see his loneliness. Then she turned and trotted off into the winter woods.

The hunter went home to his wigwam empty-handed. That night he was hungry. But he would hunt again tomorrow. The hunter was not afraid of hunger.

In the night the wind rose, and the wigwam trembled. Sleet rattled against the bark wall. The hunter sighed and rolled over and went to sleep in his warm bearskin. He was not afraid of cold, or storms.

Only one thing almost frightened the hunter. That was loneliness. He was free in the great, winter woods, but he was always alone.

Next morning he woke up hungry. He glanced around the empty wigwam and sighed. "I wish . . ." he said aloud. And then he was silent, for the sound of his voice startled him.

The hunter went to visit his traps. One trap held a fat beaver. The hunter smiled. Here was a fine·fur and a good supper. It was dark when the hunter returned to his camp. As he came toward his wigwam he saw a light. Firelight glowed through the chinks in the bark walls of his wigwam.

He thought, "The wigwam is on fire!" When he came nearer, the fire was no brighter and all was quiet. He took off his snowshoes and stood them in the snow. He lifted the deerskin curtain and entered the wigwam.

A cheerful fire burned on the little hearth. A kettle filled with nuts hung over the fire. Someone had thrown out the old spruce boughs from the bed and spread new ones. The someone was gone and the hunter was alone.

Next morning the woods gleamed in cold sunshine. The hunter laced on his snowshoes and went hunting. At dark he came home with a hare for his supper. Again, light glowed through the chinks in the bark wall. The fire was lit and beaver meat cooked in the kettle, but there was no one in the wigwam.

Next day the hunter found a mink in one of his traps. Mink fur brings a high price. "I am rich," he thought, and he wished he had a friend to share his wealth.

That night the fire was burning and supper cooked. The hunter was surprised to see a woman sitting by the fire.

She did not speak. Her brown eyes glowed. She smiled at him and served his supper in a birchbark dish.

For the rest of the winter the hunter was happy. He did not sigh again, or say "I wish." The woman became his wife. She kept the wigwam neat and warm. She dressed game, gathered wood and cooked meat but never ate the meat she cooked. She never spoke. Her face was long, heavy and homely, but her brown eyes were always soft and kind.

Spring came, and the hunter packed his furs into a bundle and made ready to go home to his village. Then, for the first time, his wife spoke. She said, "I will wait for you here."

The hunter said, "My old father will be happy to see you. Come home with me."

The wife refused. "Remember me," she warned him. "Do not marry another woman."

So the hunter took his fur pack and strode away. In the evening he came to his village. His old father was happy to see him. He counted the furs, and shouted for joy.

"You are rich," he cried. "Now you must marry. Find yourself a wife."

The hunter walked around the village and looked at the young women. He stopped to watch the chief's daughter. She sat outside her father's lodge, working colored quills into a new shirt. She looked up at the hunter and smiled. The hunter turned away.

As the summer passed the hunter grew lonely for his wife. He was glad to see the leaves turn red. Early on the morning of the first snowfall he took up his bow, his arrows and snowshoes. He said good-bye to his father, and went back into the woods.

That evening he came to his wigwam. Red light glowed through the chinks in the bark wall. The hunter lifted the deerskin curtain and entered the wigwam.

His wife sat beside the fire. She did not speak. She smiled and served his supper. While he ate, the hunter looked at the newborn boy sitting in his wife's lap. The child had his mother's soft, brown eyes. When the hunter had finished his supper the baby slid off his mother's lap. He took the dish from his father and carried it away. He wobbled as he walked, but he walked. Never before had the hunter seen a newborn child walk.

That winter was a happy time. With his little son's help the hunter took many furs. In the spring his bundle was very large.

"Come with me," he said to his wife. "Help me carry my furs." But she refused. "Remember me," she warned, "do not marry another woman."

So the hunter went home alone to his father. "You are rich," the old man cried. "You have trapped enough for two men."

The village hummed with talk of the hunter's wealth. One day the chief came to see him. "You are rich," said the chief, "but you are not married. Marry my daughter."

The chief's daughter held her head high and smiled at the hunter. He saw pride in her face and hardness in her eyes. Very politely, he refused to marry the chief's daughter.

Fall came again. As the air grew colder the hunter's heart grew lighter. On the morning of the first snow he left the village, and returned joyfully to his wigwam.

The winter wife sat beside the fire. She smiled and served the hunter his supper. Her son sat beside her. A new baby son sat in her lap.

When the hunter had finished supper, the baby took the dish and carried it away. He wobbled on weak, new legs, but the hunter knew that soon he would be strong.

That winter, with both his sons' help, the hunter took more furs than ever before. In the spring, his bundle was almost too heavy to carry. He said to his wife, "Help me carry my furs home." She refused.

Bent under the heavy pack, the hunter took two days to stumble home. His old father danced around the pack and sang for joy. Then he said, "My son, you are the richest man in the village. If you will marry the chief's daughter, I will have a rich, powerful family beside me."

And so the chief's daughter became the hunter's summer wife. She did not know that. She thought she was his only wife. She embroidered a new shirt for him so he could walk proudly through the village.

But as the fall came nearer the hunter grew uneasy. He feared that his summer wife would want to go with him to the winter woods. He warned her that the winter woods were lonely.

"I will not be lonely," she said. "My father and your father are coming too."

Snow fell. With a heavy heart, the hunter led his summer family through the woods to his wigwam. When they came near, they saw red light glowing through the bark wall.

The summer wife cried, "Your wigwam is on fire!" She ran ahead and lifted the deerskin curtain.

There sat the winter wife with her sons and a newborn daughter. The summer family and the winter family stared at one another. The hunter looked down at the snow.

The summer wife cried, "You never told me you had another wife."

Very softly, the hunter answered, "I have no other wife."

The winter wife heard his words. She came out of the wigwam and faced the summer wife. "I leave you my children," she said, "but you must be kind to them." Then she vanished. The three children remained. The summer wife walked into the wigwam and pushed them away from the fire.

The hunter spent the next days setting traps. His sons and his fathers helped him. The little girl helped the summer wife build a new wigwam.

"Your daughter is strong," the summer wife told the hunter, "but she will not eat meat. That is why she is so thin."

That night the hunter dreamed that the little girl woke her brothers. "I am hungry," she whispered. "My hands hurt from work. I cannot live here anymore. I want my mother."

"Come," said the oldest boy, "we will find our mother." And in his dream the hunter watched his son push a hole through the bark wall. The hunter saw moonlight outside, silver on snow. The hole darkened as the children crept through it. The hunter saw them walking away in the moonlight. Then they began to skip and jump. Their shapes changed, and three young moose trotted away from the wigwam.

In the morning the summer wife woke the hunter. "Your children are gone," she said happily.

The hunter jumped up and pulled on his leggings. "Tell my father I have gone after the children," he said. He laced on his snowshoes, took his ax, and hurried away on the track of the three young moose.

For three days the hunter followed the moose tracks. He found snow beds and stripped trees. On the third day the snow sparkled in the tracks. The hunter knew he was close to the moose.

At sunset he stood under a maple tree and looked out across a bright clearing. Two young bull moose stood in the clearing. They looked in the hunter's face and did not run away. A fuzzy calf lay resting in the snow. Beyond her, a big cow moose rose to her feet. She twitched her hairy ears, and looked at the hunter with kind brown eyes.

The hunter took his ax and drove it into the maple tree. He took off his snowshoes and stood them beside the tree. The ax and the snowshoes were a message to his old father.

He walked up to the cow and touched her soft nose. "Forgive me, Winter Wife," he said, "and let me stay with you forever."

The hunter's head grew heavy, and huge antlers branched from it. His shoulders humped. Strength flowed through four new legs.

Five moose wandered together, away from the clearing. Together, they drifted like shadows through the darkening winter woods.